SPLINTERS

(THIS GIRL NEEDS A MIRACLE.....)

KEVIN SYLVESTER

TUNDRA BOOKS

Published in Canada by Tundra Books,
75 Sherbourne Street, Toronto, Ontario M5A 2P9

Published in the United States by Tundra Books of Northern New York,
P.O. Box 1030, Plattsburgh, New York 12901

Library of Congress Control Number: 2009937951

Library and Archives Canada Cataloguing in Publication

Sylvester, Kevin
Splinters / Kevin Sylvester.

For ages 6-8.
ISBN 978-0-88776-944-3

I. Title.

PS8637.Y42S94 2010   jc813'.6   C2009-905770-0

We acknowledge the financial support of the Government of Canada through the Book Publishing
Industry Development Program (BPIDP) and that of the Government of Ontario through
the Ontario Media Development Corporation's Ontario Book Initiative. We further acknowledge the
support of the Canada Council for the Arts and the Ontario Arts Council for our publishing program.

ONTARIO ARTS COUNCIL
CONSEIL DES ARTS DE L'ONTARIO

Medium: watercolor and pencil on Arches paper
Design: Jennifer Lum
Printed in China

1 2 3 4 5 6   15 14 13 12 11 10

To my family, especially Mum and Dad,
who drove me to a lot of early hockey games!

ACKNOWLEDGMENTS

The author would like to acknowledge the support of the Ontario Arts Council
and to thank all the hockey players at Bill Bolton Arena.

Cindy Winters loved hockey.

Hockey made her feet tingle, her hands twitch, and her heart race.

Cindy wanted to play all the time, and sometimes she got her wish.

She and her parents lived in a dingy old basement, in a dingy old house.

One day the basement got so cold the pipes burst, and the dingy old floor froze over. Cindy played until her skates wore right through to the concrete.

Cindy wanted only one more thing: to play on a real team. "With real teammates," she said to herself as she lay on her mattress behind the old furnace, "and a real uniform and a real goal . . . not just a couple of old rubber boots."

Hockey leagues cost a lot. Cindy's parents worked hard just to pay the rent and buy food. Cindy was not going to ask them for help – she was determined to get the money herself. *It's just like being on the ice*, she thought. *Sometimes you have to go around all five players to score.*

Most of the time, Cindy played on frozen ponds. She was good and would score goals so easily that it sometimes seemed she was magic.

Cindy sold hot chocolate and cold lemonade. She delivered newspapers and groceries. She raked leaves and walked her elderly neighbor's dog. Finally, after what seemed forever, she had saved enough quarters and pennies to sign up for a real league.

Cindy hauled her mother's old equipment from underneath the stairs and headed to the rink.

At her very first practice, she met the Blister Sisters.

They could tell she was one good hockey player, and they were jealous.

They insulted her old equipment.

"Look at that moldy junk!"

"What century are *those* skates from?"

Then they made her look bad on the ice. They tripped her and knocked her into the boards. They would pass the puck way ahead of Cindy, then blame her for being too slow.

They could do this because their mom was the coach.

Before long, Coach Blister told Cindy to sit on the bench. "It's made of wood – try not to get any splinters," she sneered. "You've been making my daughters look bad. Now watch them. Maybe you'll learn something."

"But I want to play," Cindy said.

"Such attitude!" Coach Blister replied. "From now on, you'll clean their uniforms and tape their sticks."

When Cindy showed up for the first game, the twins had left her a present.

Cindy spent the entire game watching from the bench.

"I'll never get to show how good I am," Cindy said to herself. She didn't play in the next game, or the next, or the next.

One day, Cindy saw a notice on the arena billboard:

Tryouts will be held tomorrow

for

an all-star hockey team.

Each team is allowed to send its two best players.

One player from each team will be chosen by

Head Coach Charmaine Prince.

"Charmaine Prince!" Cindy said. "She's won every trophy there is!" Her heart soared.

But her spirits fell just as fast. "I know which two players Coach Blister will send."

And, sure enough, the sisters were already boasting about how they were going to become superstars.

"And we'll need our equipment to be especially clean, Splinters," they said.

The next day, Cindy got up and dressed in her old equipment.

She imagined she was going to the tryouts.

 She imagined the Blisters laughing.

 Despite her best efforts to stay cheerful, a tear rolled down her cheek.

 Suddenly, the basement became very, very cold.

 Cindy heard music, like an old pipe organ.

Looking up, she saw an old woman, not more than two feet tall, hovering in the air. She was wearing a mask and old leather goalie pads.

"Who . . . who are you?" Cindy asked.

"Why, I am your fairy goaltender," the woman replied.

Cindy's mouth fell open.

"I've come to help you, Cindy – help you prove that you're the best player on your team."

"But the tryouts are about to start, and the rink is across town.
Nobody is going to let me on the ice in this getup."

"All easily fixed," said the fairy.

And, with a graceful swing, the fairy slashed Cindy across the leg with her magic hockey stick.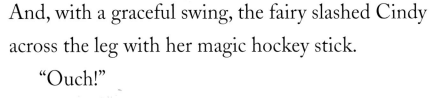

"Ouch!"

Cindy looked down. She was wearing the most stunning white-and-gold uniform. Her pants were so new, they glistened.

And there, upon her feet, was a new pair of smooth white leather skates.

"Not glass?" asked Cindy.

"Not very practical for hockey," said the fairy. "Now look outside."

In the driveway stood a sparkling new Zamboni.

"You better jump on if you want to get to the rink on time. But, remember," warned the fairy, "the spell ends when the final buzzer sounds. You must be off the ice."

"I understand," said Cindy, "and thank you."

Cindy arrived just a few minutes after tryouts started. She slipped onto the bench beside Coach Prince, who didn't seem happy. "They're all good," she whispered to her assistant, "but I don't see a star out there."

Cindy slid past her onto the ice.

Cindy began skating between all the pylons: backwards, forwards, crossing over both ways. She took the puck cleanly on every pass and passed the puck perfectly in every drill.

Coach Prince was stunned. She counted the girls. "She's not on my list," she said. But Coach Prince couldn't believe her luck. *What a player!*

Coach Prince decided to put her new players through a real test.

A game.

She picked the twenty best players and dropped the puck.

Cindy was chosen for team one. The Blister Sisters, for once, were on the other team.

Cindy was terrific, swooping when the other players swiped, weaving in and out, scoring, setting up goals.

The Blisters' team was also very good, and with time winding down, the game was tied 7-7.

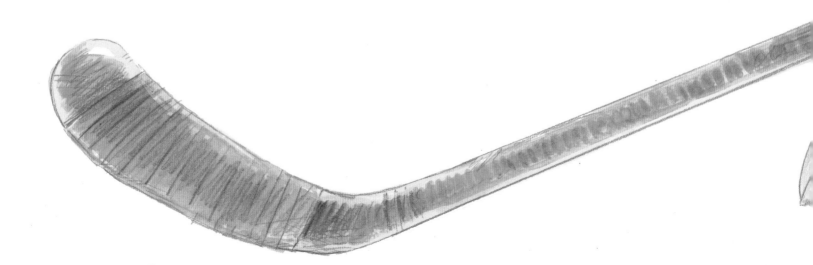

Cindy was still on the ice. She was having so much fun that she forgot about her fairy goaltender's warning.

The clock counted down the final seconds of the tryouts.

10 . . .

Cindy stole the puck behind her own net.

9 . . .

She sped up the ice.

8 . . .

She swooped around three players. But something was starting to happen.

7 . . .

She could feel her equipment shrinking and her laces unraveling.

6 . . .

It was just the Blisters between her and the net.

5 . . .

Cindy faked a shot and sped past the sisters. But they hooked her with their sticks.

4 . . .

A stick caught her foot.

3 . . .

Cindy glanced back and saw one of her skates slide off her foot. She stumbled, but as she fell, she lifted the puck up and into the top corner of the net.

GOAL!

The other girls let out a loud cheer and
rushed toward her.

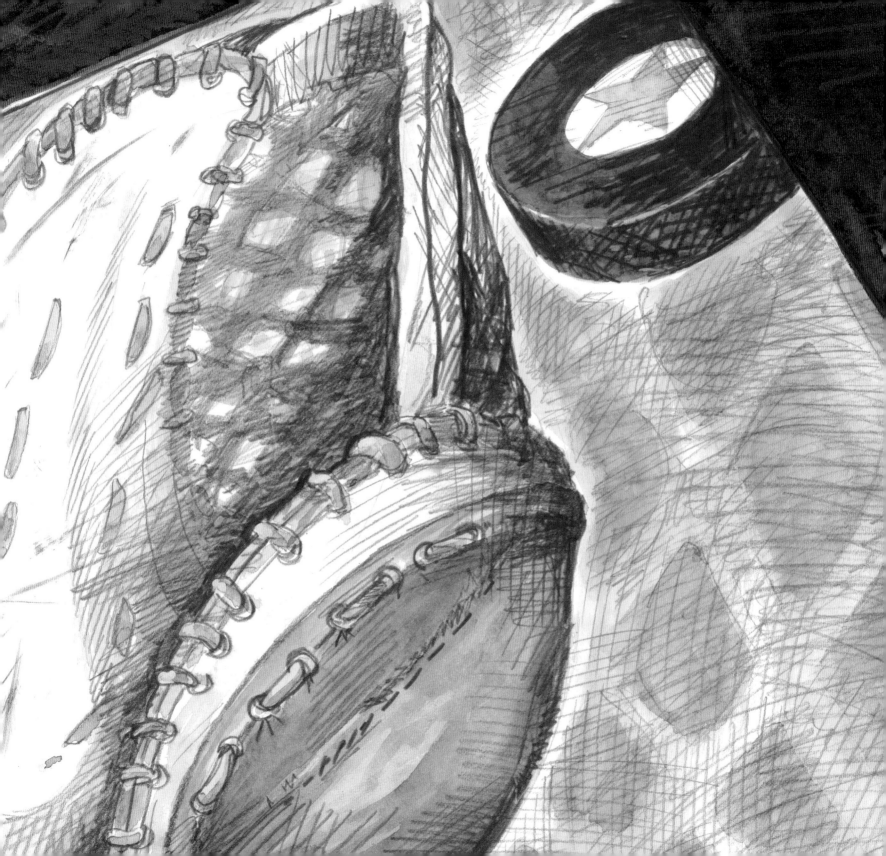

Cindy looked back to where her skate had fallen.

2 . . .

There was no time to go back for it. She had to get away.

1 . . .

The Zamboni door opened a crack.

Cindy slipped through just as the buzzer hit zero.

She looked down and saw that she was the same old Splinters, except for one shiny skate.

She quickly hid herself behind a pillar. The rest of the team rushed into the hallway and right past her.

The next morning at practice, everyone was talking about the mysterious superstar.

"Coach Prince says she won't announce the team until she finds her."

"Oh?" Cindy's ears perked up.

The Blister Sisters also paid close attention.

"Yes, the girl left behind one of her skates. Coach Prince plans to search everywhere to find the girl who fits that skate."

The Blisters looked at each other and
smiled. They hatched a plan.

Coach Prince went from locker room to
locker room, trying the skate on every girl she
could find. Finally, she came to Cindy's rink.

But Cindy wasn't there. Coach Blister had
ordered her out of the room and told her not
to come back until she had new tape and pucks
for every player on the team.

At the same time, the Blister Sisters put their own plan into action. Just before Coach Prince arrived, they stomped on the feet of every other player on the team. By the time they finished, every player had toes so swollen that there was no way they could try on the skate.

The Blister Sisters said they'd love to try it on.

Well, try as they might, the sisters couldn't get the skate on. They pushed and they pulled and grunted and groaned, but it was no use.

"That's it," said Coach Prince. "I've tried it on every girl in this city. Maybe I should just give up and pick the team anyway."

Cindy walked into the room, sagging under the weight of forty rolls of tape and three buckets of pucks. She dropped them as soon as she spotted Coach Prince. The pucks fell on the Blisters' toes. "Is she on the team?" asked Coach Prince. The twins snorted. "Splinters? That clumsy slob? She can't even afford decent skates. There's no way she'd have a skate as nice as that one."

But Coach Prince insisted. "I intend to try the skate on every girl." She asked Cindy to sit down and slipped the skate on her foot.

It went on as if it had been custom-made . . . which, of course, it had.

For once, the twins were speechless. And their jaws practically smacked their knees when Cindy pulled the other skate out of her duffel bag and put it on.

Out of nowhere, her fairy goaltender appeared and slashed her again with her magic hockey stick.

"Ouch!"

Cindy's old clothes transformed into the finest hockey equipment anywhere. The Blisters instantly recognized the star of the tryouts, and they were hopping mad. "She wasn't invited! She's not on your list! It's not fair!"

But Coach Prince pulled Cindy aside. "How would you like to be the captain of my new team?"

Cindy could hardly believe it. She hugged Coach Prince and grabbed her duffel bag. "I'd love it!" she said.

They walked out arm in arm. They were both so happy, they didn't even notice the temper tantrums behind them, as the Blister Sisters yelled and screamed and cracked their sticks over each other's head.

Cindy and Coach Prince knew they were both going to love hockey happily ever after.